For Eve and Jack
(not the one in the book),
with thanks for their
support and kindness of
gigantic proportions
E.W.

For Jade & Eva
B.D.

First published 2015 by
Macmillan Children's Books,
This edition published 2018 by
Macmillan Children's Books
an imprint of Pan Macmillan,
20 New Wharf Road, London N1 9RR.
Associated companies throughout the world.
www.panmacmillan.com
ISBN: 978-1-5290-0592-9
Text © Elli Woollard 2015
Illustrations © Benji Davies 2015
Moral rights asserted. All rights reserved.
A CIP catalogue record for this book is
available from the British Library.
2 4 6 8 9 7 5 3 1
Printed in China

THE Giant OF JUM

ELLI
WOOLLARD

BENJI
DAVIES

MACMILLAN CHILDREN'S BOOKS

The Giant of Jum was a grumpy old grouch
who was constantly grizzling and grumbling.
And when he was hungry he'd slobber and slouch
and say, "Oh how my tummy is rumbling!"

"Fee!" he said and, "Fi!" he said and, "Fo!" he said and, "Fum!
How I pine, how I wish for a child on a dish.
Little children are yummy yum yum!"

And he thought of a tale that his brother had told
of a beanstalk and boy known as Jack.

'He'd be nice', thought the Giant, 'if eaten quite cold
with a side dish of beans for a snack'.

He strode through the land with such thunderous stomps that the trees started shaking and swaying.

Through fields and forests, through rivers and swamps and to gardens where children were playing.

"Fum!" he said and, "Fo!" he said and, "Fi!" he said and, "Fee!
Children, I feel, make a fabulous meal.
I will gobble you up for my tea!"

But the children said, "What a magnificent man!
You're so marvellously magic and tall!"
And they said, "Will you help us? We're sure that you can.
Oh please will you fetch us our ball?"

The Giant said, "Well, I suppose it won't hurt,
but soon, have no fear, I'll be back.
You'd be scrumptious if eaten with cream for dessert
just as soon as I've gobbled that Jack."

"Fo!" he said and, "Fum!" he said and, "Fee!" he said and, "Fi!
Children taste nice mixed with pasta or rice
and they're perfect when popped in a pie!"

But the children ran up and they yelled, "Look at that!
Up there in the leaves — can you see?

Oh please will you help us and rescue our cat?
It's got stuck up that sycamore tree."

The Giant said, "Well, I suppose it won't hurt,
but soon, have no fear, I'll be back.
You'd be scrumptious if eaten with cream for dessert
just as soon as I've gobbled that Jack."

"Fi!" he said and, "Fee!" he said and, "Fum!" he said and, "Fo!
My very best treat is some children to eat.
I will start at the littlest toe."

But the smallest boy whispered, "My legs are so sore!"
and he slumped to the ground and he cried.
"I can't make it home, I can't walk any more.
Oh please could you give me a ride?"

The Giant said, "Well, I suppose I don't mind,"
and he lifted the boy on his back.
The boy said, "I love you, you're wonderfully kind!
And what is your name? I'm called Jack."

"Fee!" he said and, "Fi!" he said and,
"Little Jack snack, is that right?
I'll pulp you and stew you,
I'll gulp you and chew you
and gobble you up in one bite!"

But the children said, "Oh no you wouldn't!
We think that you've made a mistake.
You're such a kind giant, you couldn't.

Nice giants always eat . . .

The Giant was starving.
His tummy was rumbling, but then he said,
"Wait, are you sure?

"I'm grizzly and grumpy and grouchy and grumbly.
I've not been called lovely before!"

"You rescued a cat from a tree," shouted Jack,
"and you fetched us our ball — you're so nice!
You gave me a ride through the streets on your back
so we've made this for you — have a slice!"

"Ho!" he said and, "Hum!" he said and, "Ha!" he said and,
"Hee!
Chocolate's much better than children!"
And he ate it all up for his tea.